FRASER

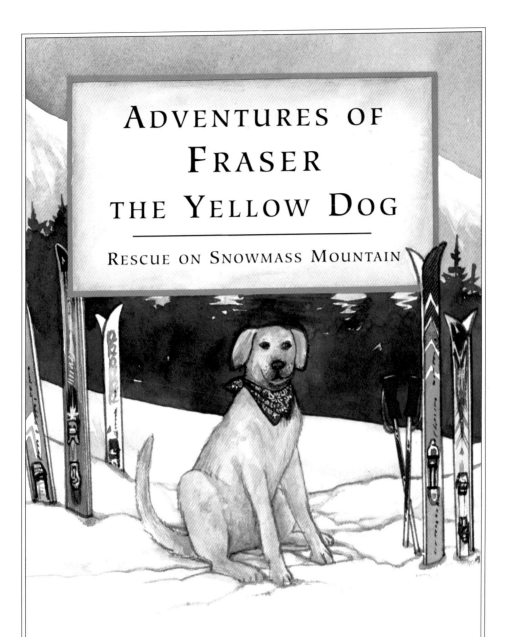

Adventures of Fraser the Yellow Dog

Rescue on Snowmass Mountain

BY JILL SHEELEY

ILLUSTRATED BY TAMMIE LANE

COURTNEY PRESS

First edition published in 1996 by Courtney Press, Aspen, Colorado.
Copyright © 1996 by Jill Sheeley.

A very special thanks to Rob Seideman, Tammie Lane, my family and all my many friends who gave me advice and support.

The names Hanging Valley Wall, The Wall, K-T Gully, Lower Powderhorn, AMF, The Cirque, No. 12 High Alpine Chairlift, Wall 1, Strawberry Patch, and High Alpine Restaurant are the property of Aspen Skiing Company, L.L.C., and are used with its permission.

"Your Responsibility Code" is officially endorsed by the National Ski Areas Association. Permission was granted to reprint "The Code" in this book.

This is a fictional story. The snow slide that occurs in the story does so for the purpose of creating adventure.

Library of Congress Catalog Card Number: 96-86547

For information about ordering this book, write: Jill Sheeley, P.O. Box 845, Aspen, CO 81612.

Printed in Korea.
ISBN 0-9609108 3-2

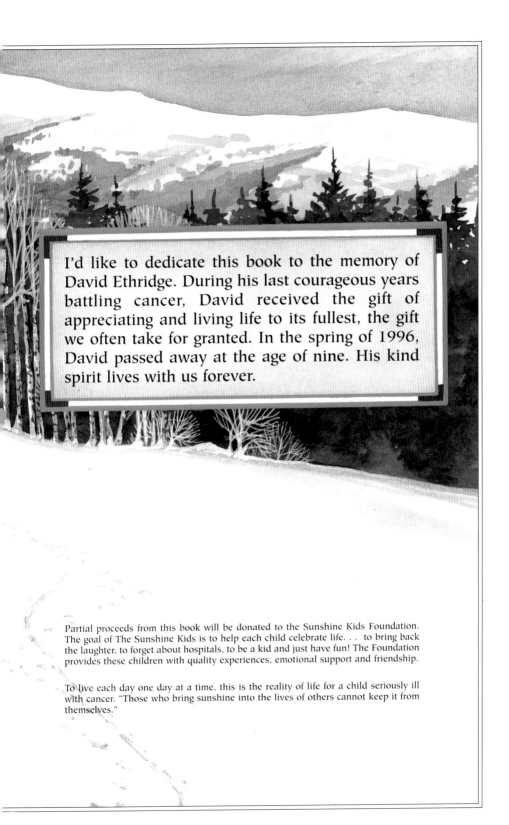

I'd like to dedicate this book to the memory of David Ethridge. During his last courageous years battling cancer, David received the gift of appreciating and living life to its fullest, the gift we often take for granted. In the spring of 1996, David passed away at the age of nine. His kind spirit lives with us forever.

Partial proceeds from this book will be donated to the Sunshine Kids Foundation. The goal of The Sunshine Kids is to help each child celebrate life. . . to bring back the laughter, to forget about hospitals, to be a kid and just have fun! The Foundation provides these children with quality experiences, emotional support and friendship.

To live each day one day at a time, this is the reality of life for a child seriously ill with cancer. "Those who bring sunshine into the lives of others cannot keep it from themselves."

Courtney was grinning. "I'm dying to ski Hanging Valley Wall," she said.

"Do you think we should," asked Katy, "after that humungous storm last night?"

"Sounds good to me," said Taylor. "The Wall's steep and deep!"

Fraser whined. He wanted to go, too.

"Fraser, you know we'd love to take you with us," Courtney said, "but dogs aren't allowed. We'll be back soon." Courtney grabbed one of her dad's long climbing ropes, and tied Fraser to a post. She left him fresh water and some food. Then she gave him a big kiss good-bye.

After skiing several easy runs to warm up their legs, the girls decided to ski some more difficult runs: K-T Gully, Lower Powderhorn, AMF, and The Cirque. The bumps were soft with the layer of fresh snow. The girls were enjoying themselves and feeling confident.

Riding up the fast-moving chairlift, the girls could smell juicy hamburgers grilling. The smoke filled the air.

"Wow," said Aime, "I'm starving. Let's stop for lunch at High Alpine. We can sit outside on the deck."

The girls had worked up quite an appetite. They wolfed down grilled cheese sandwiches and French fries. The noonday sun warmed them as they rested and chatted.

After lunch, Courtney was ready. "Let's ski The Wall now," she told her friends. "We can ski all the way down and play with Fraser."

The girls were in great spirits. Snuggled together on the No. 12 chairlift, they sang *"I've been working on the railroad..."* At the top of High Alpine lift, they popped out of their skis, slung them over their shoulders, and hiked for ten minutes before reaching The Wall.

"Awesome!" the girls screamed. The views were spectacular.

With their hair blowing wildly in the wind, the girls took off skiing, whooping and hollering as they tackled the most challenging run on Snowmass Mountain. The air was cold, but the sun warmed their chilly noses. They schussed together down a narrow chute surrounded by two cliffs. Courtney yelled to her friends, "I'm going over to ski Strawberry Patch. I'll meet you at the bottom." The other girls continued straight down. Courtney stopped for a quick rest, and stood for a moment in awe of the valley's silence.

Picking her way in and around the trees, Courtney whizzed down Strawberry Patch. Suddenly, out of nowhere, she heard a sound rise from the earth...**WHOOMF!** She felt the ground move underneath her. From above, clumps of heavy snow moved quickly, totally surrounding her.

Courtney tried to ski toward the nearest tree for safety, but the sea of flowing snow moved faster than she could. The snow buried one leg, then the other. As quickly as this slide began, it stopped. Courtney tried to move, but couldn't. Her heart was pounding. She was in trouble.

Her dad had been a ski patrolman, and warned Courtney of the dangers of being caught in a snowslide. She could still hear his voice, strong and powerful inside her head. "If you're ever buried in snow, you must try to stay calm. Think good thoughts."

Courtney closed her eyes and took several deep breaths. She pictured in her mind where she would like to be: in her log home with her mom and dad, her black cat, Scratchy, her collie, Abby, and her beloved yellow dog, Fraser.

Soon Courtney was floating above the ski slopes, swept away in a dream. In her dream, Courtney could take Fraser everywhere with her: to school…

Ice skating...

Trapeze class...

Sailing...

Suddenly, Courtney was awakened to a whimpering sound and many wet licks on her cold face.

"Fraser," she said, "it's you! I'm not dreaming. How did you ever find me?" Fraser barked loudly as he began digging the snow away from Courtney.

Then Courtney heard voices shouting out her name. "I'm here!" she yelled. "I'm over here!"

Within minutes, two ski patrolmen arrived, equipped with shovels, first-aid gear and blankets. It didn't take long for the two strong patrolmen to free Courtney from the heavy snow.

"Thank you so much for saving me," Courtney said.

"We didn't save you," replied one of the patrolman, "your dog did."

Courtney looked at Fraser, who stood proudly by her side. Katy was breathing heavily, "When you didn't show up at the bottom of The Wall, we got worried and called the ski patrol. We've been searching for you ever since."

The patrolman said, "Then we heard a dog barking and followed the sound. That's one smart dog!" Courtney held Fraser close to her chest. "How about a ride in the toboggan?" the patrolman asked.

When they arrived at the bottom of the mountain, Courtney's dad was there to greet her.

"Thanks for the good advice, Dad," Courtney said. "It came in handy." Then she hugged Fraser. "Thanks again for rescuing me today, Fraser. I'm going to take you out for your favorite treat."

The next day, after a very good night's rest, Courtney took Fraser to Boogie's Diner for an ice-cream sundae!

"You're the best dog a girl could ever have," she said. "I wonder what our next adventure will be?"

Your
Responsibility Code

Skiing can be enjoyed in many ways. Always show courtesy to others and be aware that there are elements of risk in skiing that common sense and personal awareness can help reduce. Observe the code listed below and share with other skiers the responsibility for a great skiing experience.

1 Always stay in control and be able to stop or avoid other people or objects.

2 People ahead of you have the right of way. It is your responsibility to avoid them.

3 You must not stop where you obstruct a trail or are not visible from above.

4 Whenever starting downhill or merging into a trail, look uphill and yield to others.

5 Always use devices to help prevent runaway equipment.

6 Observe all posted signs and warnings. Keep off closed trails and out of closed areas.

7 Prior to using any lift, you must have the knowledge and ability to load, ride and unload safely.

Ski safely and have fun!